WITHDRAWN

For Olli, Paddy, Ozzy, and Kaisa —T.T.
For my little boys Sam and Tom —A.R.

First American edition published in 2013 by Andersen Press USA, an imprint of Andersen Press Ltd.
www.andersenpressusa.com

First published in Great Britain in 2012 by Andersen Press Ltd.,
20 Vauxhall Bridge Road, London SW1V 2SA.
Published in Australia by Random House Australia Pty.,
Level 3, 100 Pacific Highway, North Sydney, NSW 2060.

Distributed in the United States and Canada by
Lerner Publishing Group, Inc.
241 First Avenue North, Minneapolis, MN 55401 U.S.A.
www.lernerbooks.com

Color separated in Switzerland by Photolitho AG, Zürich.
Printed and bound in Malaysia by Tien Wah Press.

Library of Congress Cataloging-in-Publication Data is available.
ISBN: 978-1-4677-1143-2

1 - TWP - 7-6-12
This book has been printed on acid-free paper.

THE PETS YOU GET!

Thomas Taylor

Adrian Reynolds

ANDERSEN PRESS USA

My sister's got a guinea pig.
It's her little furry friend.
She loves it because it's cuddly,
and she never stops hugging it!

But me, I think a guinea pig is really boring. It's nowhere near as cool as other pets you can get! Like a . . .

... dog! Much more exciting and much more fun!

He can bark.
He can jump.
He can run.

We'd have such a great time splashing about on the beach.

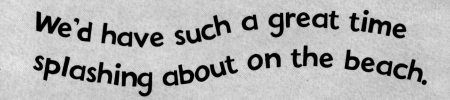

Then we'd snooze together on the sand.

But my sister says that dogs are smelly
and make a lot of mess...

...while guinea pigs are tidy and don't
make any noise while you're watching TV.

They're so boring!
But if she won't have a dog, then
I know the perfect pet. It's a . . .

...huge shaggy brown bear!
With claws and teeth and a ferocious roar!
If I had a bear, we'd crash around the
woods all day long...

...and then watch the sun go down from his mountain cave.

But my sister says a bear would be too big for her bed. She'd rather sleep with her cuddly little guinea pig instead.

Nah! *I* don't want a pet that sleeps for half the day. I need something much more exciting. The pet I'd *really* like to get is a . . .

... huge smoking dragon!

With wings and horns and fire from his nose!

That would show my sister!

But my sister says that dragons don't exist
and that I'm just being silly.

Then she gives her guinea pig a
big kiss, right in front of me!

Yuck! So gross! Why would you want a silly little guinea pig when there are so many more AMAZING pets you can get? Like . . .

...prowling **panthers** or roaring **polar** bears or **eagles** or rhinos or humongous stomping **dinosaurs!**

Or a tentacled sea monster or a hulking gorilla or a **snake** or a **rat** or even a **giant cat** . . . any one would make a great pet for me!

But my sister just smiles and says
I should give her guinea pig a try.
She pops him on my knee and . . .

. . . he runs up
my arm with his
sharp claws!

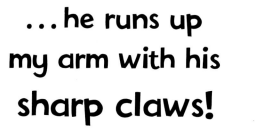

Then he **leaps** and slides down and zooms off across the ground.

And dashes away with one of my toys in his **toothy jaws!**

So we chase him, wherever he peeks out, wherever we hear his funny little squeak.

And he's really hard to catch!

What a fantastic game of hide-and-seek!

In the end, I agree that guinea pigs are sometimes really fun after all. And my sister says that as long as I promise not to scare him, I can share him.

And I say yes . . .

...though I'd still like a dragon someday!